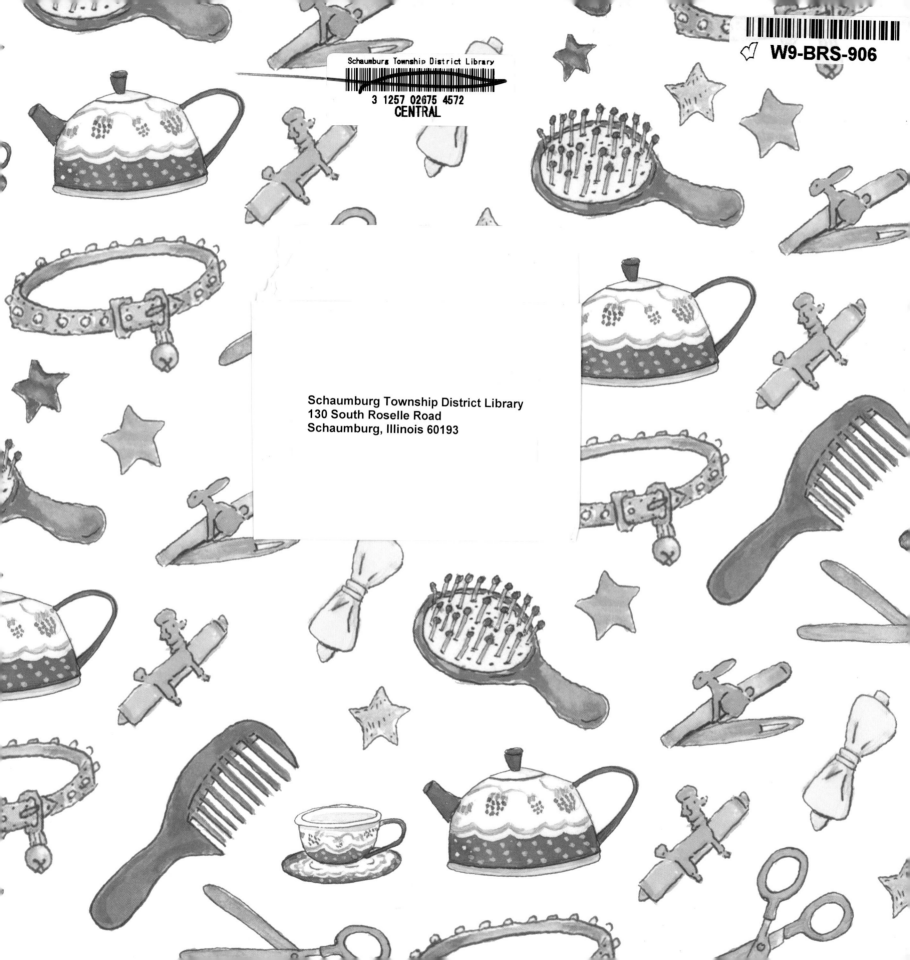

Big Little Mother

Thank you Mary Ludington for all your work and beautiful self. The amazing Shannon Pennefeather and the Borealis A-Team: Pam McClanahan, Dan Leary, Alison Aten, Mary Poggione. Superstar Chris Monroe. Lynda Barry, Betty Tisel, and Collette Morgan. And my incredible, understanding family: Dora, Lavon, Laura, Steven.

— K K

Thank you Dann Edholm, Scott Lunt, Nancy Spellerberg, Larry Monroe, Mickey Sweere, Meghann Jones, Dan Leary, all the fine folks at Borealis Books, and, of course, the inimitable Kevin Kling.

— C M

Borealis Books is an imprint of the Minnesota Historical Society Press.

www.mhspress.org

The Minnesota Historical Society Press is a member of the Association of American University Presses.

Book design by Anders Hanson, Mighty Media

Manufactured in Canada

10 9 8 7 6 5 4 3 2 1

∞ The paper used in this publication meets the minimum requirements of the American National Standard for Information Sciences— Permanence for Printed Library Materials, ANSI Z39.48-1984.

INTERNATIONAL STANDARD BOOK NUMBER
ISBN: 978-0-87351-911-3 (cloth)

LIBRARY OF CONGRESS CATALOGING-IN-PUBLICATION DATA
Kling, Kevin, 1957–
Big little mother / Kevin Kling ; Chris Monroe.
pages cm
Summary: A four-year-old boy demonstrates what a good teacher his big sister is during her tap dancing class and garners praise for them both.
ISBN 978-0-87351-911-3 (cloth : alk. paper)
[1. Brothers and sisters—Fiction.] I. Monroe, Chris, illustrator. II. Title.
PZ7.K6797585Bk 2013
[E]—dc23
2013015999

BIG

Little Mother

KEVIN
KLING

CHRIS
MONROE

Before there was me, my sister had a cat.

They did everything together.

My sister dressed her in doll clothes and invited her to tea parties.

She taught her to play the piano by putting cream cheese on the keys.

One day when I was four years old
and Kittywumpus was five,
my sister declared
that Kitty had
let herself go.

Tomorrow we will give you a celebrity makeover.

That night when Dad came home from work, and opened the front door,

Kittywumpus had let herself go.

At supper
Dad says
Kittywumpus
will come home
when she is
good and ready.

So we make the
house beautiful
for her return.
We pick up
clothes, make
the beds, and
sweep the floor.

Mom is thrilled. She calls my sister "another mother."

We wait and wait and wait, but no Kittywumpus. My sister uses the time to practice a haircut on me ...

before giving one to her doll.

We play **ADVENTURES IN CARDBOARD.**

COUCH CUSHION TREASURE HUNT.

She is a beautiful dancer.

We reveal nature's secrets.

Still no
Kittywumpus.

We make names for new star families.

Early the
next morning,
my sister says,

She puts me in
her doll's clothes.

And invites me to tea.

And makes
me play
the piano.

Wednesday night is tap dance.

While my sister's class dances,

I sit with Mom and the other mothers and children.

The whole class looks at me. Everyone laughs.

I stand up and ...

DANCE!

Then, the teacher turns to me.

After class
my sister hugs me.

My Masterpiece!

No more
tea parties.

You are better
than a cat.

The next day Kittywumpus comes back. Mom says she was visiting the lady down the street and must have grown tired of the good life.

Now my sister has two students,
though Kittywumpus is a year ahead of me.

Epilogue

My sister is a wonderful mother
and has been a teacher
for over thirty-five years.
I like to think of myself as her first student.